Weekly Reader Presents

Wembley Fraggle and the Magic Stone

By Louise Gikow · Pictures by Lauren Attinello

Muppet Press
Henry Holt and Company
NEW YORK

Published by Henry Holt and Company,
521 Fifth Avenue, New York, New York 10175

Library of Congress Cataloging in Publication Data
Gikow, Louise.
Wembley Fraggle and the magic stone.
Summary: Wembley wishes on a "magic stone" that he
be able to make decisions more easily, and his belief
in the wish changes his life dramatically.
[1. Decision making—Fiction. 2. Wishes—Fiction.
3. Puppets—Fiction] I. Attinello, Lauren, ill.
II. Title.
PZ7.G369Wg 1986 [E] 86-4638
ISBN: 0-8050-0069-0

Printed in the United States of America

ISBN 0-8050-0069-0

This book is a presentation of
Weekly Reader Books

Weekly Reader Books offers book clubs for children
from preschool through high school.

For further information write to:
Weekly Reader Books
4343 Equity Drive
Columbus, Ohio 43228

Weekly Reader Books offers several exciting
card and activity programs. For information,
write to WEEKLY READER BOOKS, P.O. Box 16636,
Columbus, Ohio 43216.

"I THINK I like the red. No, the blue is really nice. But the red is really . . . red."

Wembley Fraggle stood in his cave, staring at two pairs of earmuffs that hung on the wall. It was winter in Fraggle Rock, and no sensible Fraggle would go out without a hat or earmuffs.

"Just pick one," Gobo said impatiently. "We're meeting Red and Mokey in the Great Hall right away. And don't forget your skates!"

Wembley closed his eyes and reached out toward the earmuffs. He felt something soft between his fingers and opened his eyes. He had chosen the red ones.

"Maybe I should wear the blue ones after all," he
began. But Gobo grabbed him by the shoulder and
whisked him out of their cave before you could say
"Fraggle fun."

"I wish, I really *wish* it weren't so hard for me to make up my mind," Wembley said as he and Gobo trotted toward the frozen pond.

"Well, maybe you'll find a wishing stone, and your wish will come true," Gobo answered cheerfully. There was a legend in Fraggle Rock that certain stones had magical wishing powers.

Wembley perked up. "Do you think so, Gobo?"

Gobo shook his head. "I was only kidding," he said. "Everyone knows that there's no such thing as a wishing stone."

When Gobo and Wembley reached the Great Hall, Red and Mokey were already there.

"Come on, Wem! Get your skates on!" Gobo laced his up and glided off.

Wembley finished tying his skates and stood up. He put his left foot in front of his right foot. That's when he tripped over a Doozer stick on the ice. His legs started to slip, and his arms went around and around like a windmill. He reached for a ledge to steady himself and felt a bit of rock break away in his hand.

Oh, no! I wish I wouldn't fall! Wembley said to himself. Then, somehow, his feet got a grip on the ice, and he slowly slid to a stop.

"Nice going, Wembley!" Red laughed as she glided past. "I thought you were a goner."

"So did I!" Wembley shouted happily. He started to straighten his earmuffs and noticed something in his hand. It was a smooth, round stone. It had blue spots that seemed to glow from within. Wembley had never seen anything like it before.

What a neat stone, he thought, putting it in his pocket for safekeeping.

A little later, Boober came by with five mugs of hot radish cider on a tray.

"I thought some cider might keep you from catching cold," he said. "All this exercise can't possibly be good."

"Thanks, Boober!" Mokey said, taking her mug.

"I just wish mine weren't so hot," Wembley added.

Suddenly, an icicle hanging just above Wembley's head broke, and a little chunk of ice fell smack into his cup! "Hey!" Gobo chuckled. "All Wembley needs to do is wish for something, and it happens!"

Wembley just laughed. But as he and Gobo walked back to their cave, he put his hand into his pocket and felt the stone there, right next to his handkerchief.

What if this is a wishing stone? he thought. *After all, I wished I wouldn't fall, and I didn't. Then I wished my cider weren't so hot, and an icicle fell in it. Maybe I can wish for anything I want! I might even wish that I could make up my mind!*

"Hey, Wembley," Gobo said, interrupting Wembley's daydream. "Do you want to roast some radishes or go over to the Slide?"

For a moment, Wembley couldn't decide. But he held the stone tight. Then, somehow, he knew. He knew just what he wanted to do!

"Let's go to the Slide!" he shouted.

The wishing stone worked!

Later that night, Mokey came to talk to Gobo in his cave.

"I'm worried about Wembley," she told him. "He was in our cave a while ago, and he kept jumping up and down and saying, 'I've decided what I'm having for my bedtime snack!' and laughing a lot. Something must be wrong."

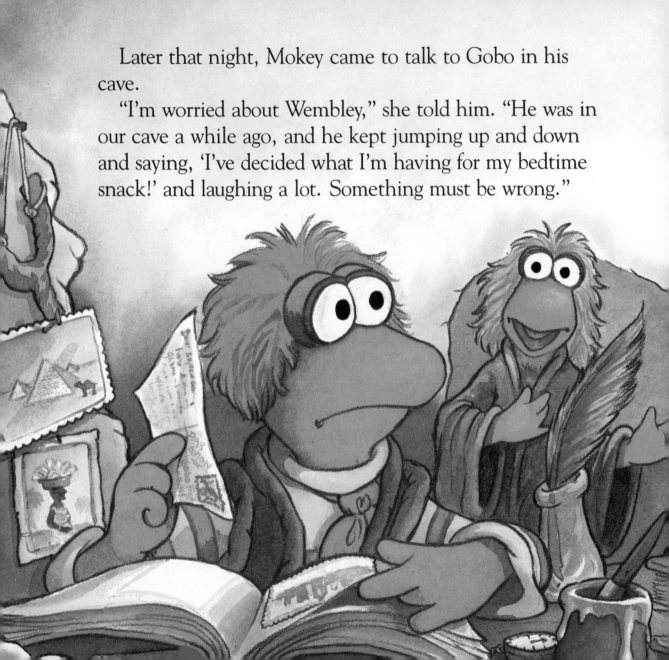

Gobo sighed. "Wembley thinks he's found a magic wishing stone. He wished he could make up his mind, and now he's making decisions all the time. He decided to have squash stew for dinner, and then he decided to go to Boober's cave for his snack. That's where he is now."

Mokey frowned. "Doesn't Wembley know that there's no such thing as a magic wishing stone?"

"I told him that, but he wouldn't believe me."

"Well, if it makes him happy . . ." Mokey said. "But I think we'd better keep an eye on him just the same."

The next morning, Wembley decided to hike to
Roaring Ravine to see the frozen waterfall.

"Wembley, I don't think this is a very good decision at
all," Gobo gasped for the third time as they climbed over
some large boulders. "It's pretty icy and dangerous in
wintertime on top of Roaring Ravine."

"That's okay!" Wembley said cheerfully. "With my
wishing stone, I'll be perfectly safe. Just don't drop
your picnic lunch."

It was a wonderful day for a hike. The weather was clear, and the wind wasn't too strong. Fraggle Rock looked beautiful, with sparkling frost and icicles everywhere. Just before lunch, they reached the deep ravine.

"Let's go this way," Wembley said confidently. "We'll get a better view of the frozen waterfall from here." He began to climb down a steep cliff.

"I don't know," Gobo said. "It looks pretty slippery, Wem—"

There was no time to say anything else. Wembley had slipped on a rock. The next thing he knew, he was hanging from a small frozen branch above the ravine. He dropped his lunch basket and watched it fall down, down, down into the ravine. It landed with a thud.

"Wembley!" Gobo yelled. "Don't move! I'm coming!"

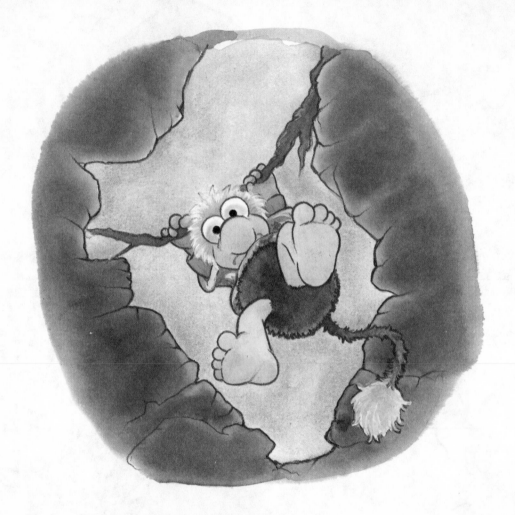

For a few moments, Wembley was too terrified to think about anything but holding on. Then he remembered the wishing stone.

"I wish," he whispered, "I wish I could climb back up to the top of the ravine."

He looked above him. But all he saw was a sheer wall of ice. Wembley couldn't move.

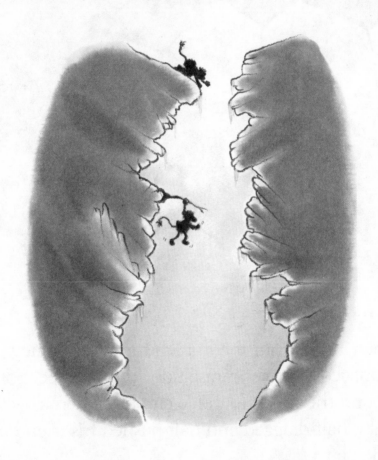

Wembley hung from the branch for a long time before Gobo managed to lower himself down on a rope. Somehow, Gobo wound the rope around Wembley. Then slowly, inch by inch, he half-dragged and half-pushed his friend up the side of the cliff.

When they reached the top, they both lay there,
frightened and out of breath. Then Wembley remembered
the wishing stone. He put his hand in his pocket and
pulled the stone out.

"Some wishing stone this turned out to be," he said
sadly. "It failed me when I needed it the most. I guess it
really isn't magic after all."

He raised his arm and threw the stone down into the ravine. It landed on the bottom, right next to his lunch.

"I knew it wasn't really magic, Wem," Gobo said gently.

"So when the icicle dropped into my cider, and when I didn't fall ice-skating—" Wembley's voice trailed off.

"It just happened that way." Gobo put his arm around his best friend's shoulders. "It wasn't magic. But you know what's better than magic? When you thought you could make decisions, you could! It didn't have anything to do with a magic stone. It had to do with you."

"It did?" Wembley asked.

"It sure did," Gobo said. "Now I'm about to show you that you can decide things for yourself without the help of any wishing stone. Wembley, what do you want to do right now?"

Wembley thought for a moment. He found it quite easy
to make up his mind.

"I want to go home!" he said happily.

So that's exactly what they did.